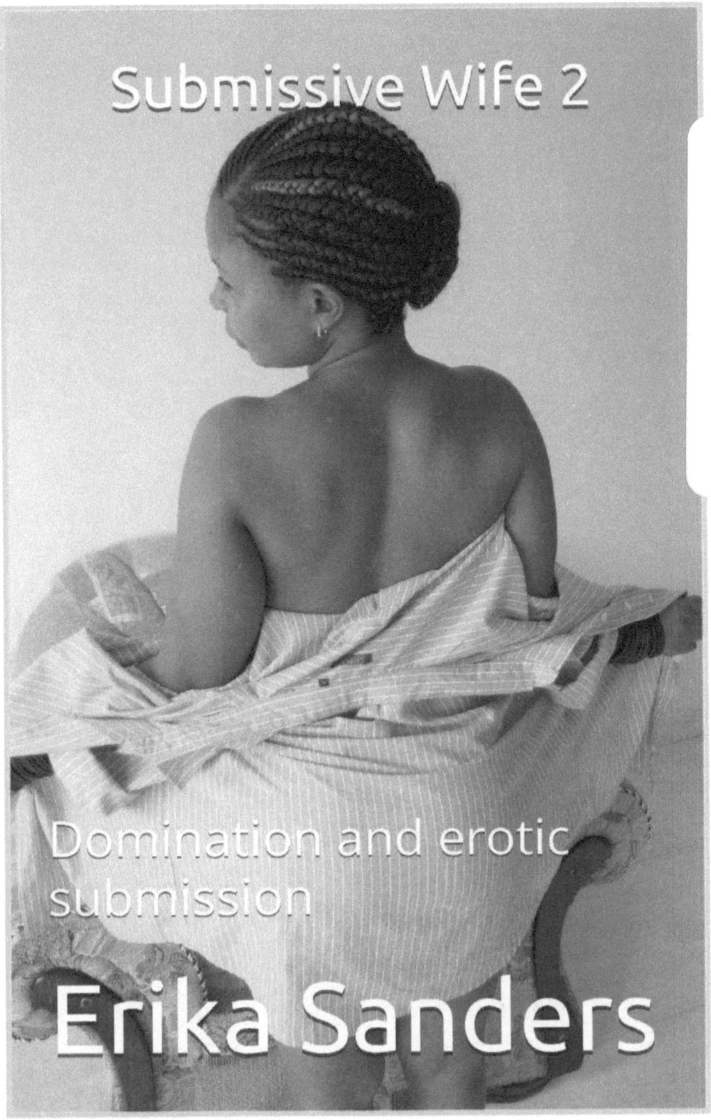

Submissive Wife 2

Domination and erotic submission

Erika Sanders

Submissive Wife 2

Erika Sanders

Domination and erotic submission
Vol. 16

Synopsis

A white wife and mother finally decides to indulge her deepest, oldest and most perverse fantasy with a black girl...

Submissive wife 2 is a story with strong erotic BDSM content and, in turn, also belonging to the Erotic Domination collection, a series of novels with high romantic and erotic BDSM content.

(All characters are 18 or older)

SUBMISSIVE WIFE 2
ERIKA SANDERS

CHAPTER I

Carefully I tuck my children into bed, pulling the blankets over their shoulders and kissing their foreheads goodnight. Gosh they look like such angels laying there falling asleep. I stand above them for a moment watching their peaceful faces and begin to envy them. Their lives are so simply at this point, not like mine. Oh did I envy them.

Turning off the lamp I slowly close the door behind me, careful not to make a sound. Moving down the hall I come upon my bedroom, where my wonderful husband lays fast asleep. I sigh contently at the sight, so glad I have a man like him. I truly am fortunate to have the family I have. To have a home like this, a wonderful car, and a good job. Yet... There has always been something missing.

Something that I've secretly craved for a long, long time. Something that I can no longer go on without trying at least one time.

With the most guilty of feelings I take my purse off the nightstand and carefully close the bedroom door. I make as little noise as possible as I move towards the front of the house. It takes a lot of courage to turn that knob, but I do.

For twenty minutes I drive through the city. Even though I know where I'm going, I still feel lost. This is a big step I'm taking. Until now it had all been in my mind. My dreams, my fantasies. All safely tucked away in the back of my twisted brain since high school. Back when 'She' first stuck it in there.

I was leaving my family behind, if only briefly, to finally realize the desires of that day so long ago.

Turning the corner I instantly see them. Young hardly dressed women of the night walking up and down the street. White, Asian, Black, or Hispanic. All competing for the attention of the various dark tinted cars passing along their sides. I remain at the corner, my car running idle as I stare at the women, looking for the one I'm here to see.

"Last chance", I whisper to myself. I still didn't have to do this. As much as my cunt was begging to push the car forward my brain was pleading for me to turn the wheel around. To go back to my kids, my husband, my home. To be a normal woman who didn't need to act out her panty drenching fantasies.

I might have actually listened to my brain if I had not seen her a moment later. The dark complexion of the girl I had come to see was unmistakable. The girl who I had been watching walk up and down these streets for almost a month. The black girl I had chosen to abuse my body tonight like the black girl in high school never did.

Turning off my brain, my foot presses on the gas. Rounding the corner I move the car closer and closer. I could clearly see she was wearing her typical street outfit. Micro skirt hugging her ass, tight pink tube top revealing every curve and bump of her breasts, and of course those shiny red high heels.

I'm almost upon her when she finally turns my way and notices the green SUV rolling along side her. Pressing fully on the breaks, the car comes to a stop just as she taps on the passenger window. With one last deep breath I press it down.

I can see the look of surprise when she sees who the driver is, clearly not expecting a woman. She takes a moment to look into the back seat to see if there is anyone else, then looks back at me.

"Looking for a good time tonight Mrs?"

I shyly nod my head, too nervous to know what else to do.

She casually opens the unlocked door and gets in. I'm amazed that I've actually gotten this far, having a prostitute inside my car. The only question left to know is if she'd actually do what I ask once I tell her. If she can look past the odd nature of my request and satisfy what I crave from her.

"In here or someplace else?"

I look at her dumbly, mentally too buzzed to react to her question.

"You want to get your freak on in the car or someplace else?"

"Someplace else." I whisper, gaining slightly my senses.

"Ok, but your paying for the room as well."

I nod, then allow her to direct me a couple blocks until we arrive at a modest looking motel complex. The whole time that I'm driving I can see her looking at me out of the corner of my eye. I can tell she's trying to figure me out and discover what game I might be playing. Why would this normal looking white woman in an SUV be requesting services from a girl like her?

While she waited outside, I went into the lobby to get a room. The guy must have seen how nervous I was as my shaking hand signed for the room and took the key from him. Thankfully he didn't bother to ask of my troubles.

CHAPTER II

Room #05 was what he had given to me. The girl was waiting right there beside me as I fumbled to unlock the door. By now she had lost her earlier curiosity about me and was impatiently waiting for me to get it all over with. For a brief moment I consider backing out, questioning the craziness of my actions. What was I doing here? Did I really need this black woman to satisfy my deepest, oldest, most perverse fantasy? Wasn't masturbation good enough anymore?

Before pushing the door open, I look back one last time and see her pretty black face. No, masturbation just wouldn't do it for me any more.

I was ever so nervous as she sat there on the bed in silence, studying me, trying to figure out if I was legit or just as crazy as I sounded. I couldn't stop from fidgeting as she stared at me from the corner of the bed, making me feel like such a fool. Who asks such things? This was wrong.

"You want me to do what?"

I knew she wouldn't immediately understand. It's so complicated, yet so childish.

"I....want you to... (I took another watery swallow) ...Dominate Me!"

Again she stared at me, probably trying to form a picture of my absurdity in her mind. It wasn't forming quickly enough.

"Well, like how?"

Gosh I was hoping she wouldn't ask too many questions. I just pay her and she'd dominate me. What's so hard to understand?

"I want you to treat me....like....(I held my breath)...dirt!"

A smile crept across her pretty young face. A smile that told me she liked what she was hearing, even if so strange. Then the smile turned to one of greater curiosity.

"Why"

"Oh please, must we discuss this? I'm willing to pay...."

"Lady, its not every day that a fancy looking white woman with an SUV asks me to treat her like dirt. What's the catch?"

Catch? This girl wants to know if there's a catch? Can't she just say yes? Can't she just agree to punish me like that black bitch in high school should have?

"Either you tell me what you really are here for, or I'm out of here!"

With that she got to her feet and made for the door.

"WAIT!" I cried after her. I didn't get this close only to get denied. "Please don't go."

She turned around and looked directly at me.

"I....have this....fantasy..."

"Yes?....."

"Its about this girl I knew back in high school. A black girl."

"Go on!" She raised an eyebrow of perked curiosity as I lowered my gaze to the floor shamefully.

"Well, she and I...well...never really got along. You see she was one of the few black girls at the school at the time and well, my girl friends and I would made fun of her incessantly."

"That doesn't sound very nice of you." She now looked a little perturbed.

"Yes well....that's what young girls do to others who don't exactly 'fit in'."

"You don't have to tell me lady. I've grown up hearing the shit you white women say behind our backs."

A tingle went up my spine at those words. I was getting slightly worried that I might offend her. Yet the look in her eyes told me I better continue explaining myself.

"I...I think I may have been the worst to her. I was always one of the first girls to start something up, making fun of her hair, her cloths, her face, her background..."

"And she just took it? She never tried to get back at you?" I could definitely sense the anger in her voice.

"No, never. Until one day that is."

The young prostitute slowly made her way back to the bed where she sat on its edge, now apparently ready to here the real reason why we were both here. She looked at me with renewed interest.

"It happened on a day that I was particularly nasty to her. My friends and I just couldn't leave her alone in one of our classes and I could tell she was both miserable and angry at us for doing so. Yet as naive as I was, I thought nothing of how enraged we were actually making her. I should have seen it coming, but I simply wasn't prepared for what she had planed after school."

I could see that she was now very much interested in my story.

"Usually my two best friends and I headed home through the fields at the back of the school. We lived not too far from there and it was usually a rather quick walk. I guess she knew we'd be going through there again that day."

"And? Did she finally teach you bitch's a lesson?"

Another shiver went through my body. I knew what the answer to her question was. I've thought about it for all of my adult life.

"No, she didn't!"

The whore just sat there looking at me, waiting for more explanation.

"Later that day, as we rounded the corner of the school, she surprised the three of us from behind. All I heard was my name being shouted, and by the time I finished turning around, a black hand had hit me HARD across my face. I saw stares as I stumbled back. The next thing I knew I was being pushed hard against a wall, her face inches away from mine. Both my friends were cowering on their knees, their cheeks red as well."

A defiant smile went from ear to ear on the black prostitute, obviously approving of the actions taken thus far by the black heroin in my story.

"I tried to fight her off, to push her away from me. But after several more slaps, I had tears in my eyes and was totally powerless. When I felt her fingers around my neck, my attention was completely hers."

"What else did she do?"

"Not much else physically. She simply held my neck tightly in her hand as she berated me. Cursing my friends and I, calling us horrible horrible names."

"Tell me what she called you girls."

"She...called us.....Stupid White Racist Cunts!

The whore nodded approvingly. I just knew my checks were red with shame.

"By the time she was done yelling, she had thoroughly assured that I would NEVER bother her again. Releasing my neck from her grasp I fell to my knees where she spat on me before storming off past my friends.

"AND?"

"And I never bothered her again."

I could see the look of disappointment in her eyes. She, like I, clearly hoped that there would be more to the story.

"So tell me lady. Why are we both in this motel room tonight?"

"Because...well...when I had fallen to my knees, my...I mean...I was....wet!" She just continued staring at me, not a change in her expression. "And...my nipples were...hard!" Still no look of change in her face. "Ever since, all I have ever thought about was that day. Her fingers around my neck with her face inches from mine, her voice pounding into my ears, my friends in tears on the floor. Gosh did she seem so powerful, so dominant over me. I felt so weak, so pathetic, so....helpless before her. Ever since I've dreamed, no...masturbated to the thoughts of what if. What if she'd decided to truly teach me a lesson for being a....'Stupid racist white cunt'? What if she would have punished me like I've fantasiesed all these years? What if? That is why I am here with you tonight. I want you to punish me like she never did."

I looked pleadingly at her, breathless form the pouring of emotional words I had just given. Yet her face the whole time remained unchanged, unmoved.

CHAPTER III

For a minute we both stared at each other. I was getting very nervous. Surely she must think I am crazy. Surely she must realize the perverse nature of my request. What woman would want another to abuse her, black or white, money or for free?

Finally a smirk came over her gorgeous face.

"Take off your blouse."

I held my breath for a moment. Did she just want me to take it off? Did this mean she was actually agreeing to do it?

The stern look on her face instinctively brought my hands up to my buttons. The whole time I was unbuttoning all I could do was look at her, trying to gain a hint of what she was thinking. My blouse fell away and landed by my feet on the floor. Her eyes immediately centering upon my bra covered chest.

"Remove it."

With an electric sigh I reached back and unclasped my bra from behind, pulling it forward and letting my pale white breasts fall free. Instantly a sly smirk appeared on her face as she gazed the size of my tits. For the first time since high school, I was feeling helpless before a black woman.

I allowed the bra to fall from my hands.

Never taking her eyes off my chest, she rose from the bed and slowly moved towards where I was standing. By now I was distinctly trembling before her.

A moan escaped my lips when her warm, soft hands cupped both fleshy orbs. I freely admit how nice it felt to be fondled this delicate way. Closing my eyes I passively stood there as I let her play with them, feeling her fingers roam, before finding their way to the center of each breast, to the rock hard nipples I knew were begging for attention. Gosh did I need this. Even with out the fantasies, I so needed it.

"Four hundred dollars." I opened my eyes and looked at her.

I had almost forgotten about this part, the negotiation. As her fingers tightened around each nipple, I was hardly in any position to disagree with her price. Numbly I nodded my head.

"You're crazy you know that?"

Again I numbly nodded my head. I surely was.

Letting go of my nipples she walked back to the edge of the bed and retook her seat upon it.

"First you pay! I don't want you complaining afterwards that I was too hard with you."

I quickly made my way over to my purse across the room. I wanted this to begin as soon as possible. As I moved my breasts jiggled quite comical I'm sure. Reaching down I picked my purse up off the chair and opened it, pulling out four crisp hundred dollar bills. Walking back over to her she took them from my hand.

"You know I will never understand you white women," she said mockingly as she held the bills up to the light, checking if they were real. "always acting as if you're the top of the gene pool," She placed the bills into her top, between her dark cleavage. "only to show up here begging to get...."

She paused in mid sentence, for the first time noticing the trembling of my body. She could see how nervous I really was.

"Are you sure you want to do this?" She asked, for the first time with a hint of compassion. I pleadingly nodded my head, looking her straight in the eyes. I needed this more than she knew.

With a sigh of indifference she told me to put my hands behind my head. My stomach was actually jerking with my failed attempts to breath normally. It was finally, actually happening. All my fantasies, all my dreams, I was finally going to live them.

With my hands clasped above my neck, my breasts lifted towards her.

"Beg!"

I blink several times at her. Beg? But...but I was paying her?

"Please, don't make me." I whimpered, realizing how much more embarrassing it would be to do so.

"No begging, no playing!"

I looked back to her face, a small tear collecting in my right eye.

"Please....Mistress, will.....you...."

"MISTRESS? HAH, no one has ever called me that before. I like it, say it again!"

"Please Mistress, will you kindly......punish me?" I looked down at my chest at the two white swaying orbs. The same two orbs my husband loves to fondle and caresses. The same breasts I've always been proud of. The same two tits that I was now offering to the hands of a twenty something black prostitute.

"Punish what Lady? What of yours would you like me to have punished?"

There was no longer any reason to hide pretenses. I was paying her to abuse my body, and it was time to tell her to do exactly that.

"My TITS, Mistress! Please punish them!"

I heard a giggle escape her lips.

"But they are such pretty white things. Why would you want to make them all red and sore?"

"Please, just hurt them!" I couldn't believe I was actually begging this much for it. Didn't she have four hundred dollars in her top for her trouble?

"Not until pretty white lady tells me why she wants a black whore to smack her cute little titties!"

"Because....because..."

"Because?"

"BECAUSE I'M A STUPID WHITE RACIST CUNT!"

(SLAP!)

The words just flowed out of my mouth magically. I didn't even think I had the guts to say them. Yet the moment I did, a gasp quickly escaped my lips as she struck my left breast with her open palm, totally unprepared for the stinging pain surging to my brain. She paused, allowing my breasts to finish jiggling about on my chest. I always knew the breasts were sensitive, but....

(WHACK)

This time, my right breast jiggled about as I bit my lower lip.

"Please, more!" I croaked.

(SLAP)....(SLAP)

The left, then the right breast went swaying as she delivered two equally forceful blows. I instinctively dropped my hands over my trebling tits, bringing them into my chest. I tried to rub the soreness out of them, but they still stung painfully. My paid tormentress sat patiently until I again placed my hands behind my head, offering my reddening tits for more of her punishment.

"Is this what's supposed to happens to racist white bitches when they cross black women? Are their big white titties supposed to get slapped to teach them a lesson?"

I numbly nodded my head.

(SLAP)(SLAP)(SLAP)(SLAP)

I moaned painfully as my knees grew weak. I struggle to remain standing with my hands behind me. The pain was unreal, but boy did I ever feel so alive!

(SLAP)(SLAP)(SLAP)(SLAP)(SLAP)

Tears were streaming down my cheeks as my tits flew every which way in tune with her swatting hands. The weight on my chest constantly shifting from the heavy abuse. I managed to close my eyes and imagine myself once again on that field. My friends on the grass in shock and tears, watching the hated black bitch grasping my neck against the wall, her hands coming across my exposed chest, teaching me the lesson I never got.

"Is this what you wanted? (SLAP) Is this what you wanted that rebelling black girl to give you? (WHACK) To humiliate you in front of your friends by smacking your fluffy white titties till you cried for more?"

"YES, MISTRESS!!!"

(SLAP)(SLAP)(SLAP)(SLAP)

I simply couldn't take anymore. The overwhelming pain finally over took me and with one final scream of despair I dropped my hands over my red sore tits and hunched over, falling to my knees in a torrent of tears.

I must have been on the floor for a good few minutes, crying and rubbing my breasts for relief. The whole time she simply sat on the edge of the bed, inspecting her nails for any damage. After a couple more minutes, I was surprised by the feeling of her hand underneath my chin, lifting it up to look again into her eyes. We stared at each other for a moment, my crying reduced to irregular snivels by the time she finally spoke.

"You deserve this don't you?"

I nodded yes.

"Stupid white bitch!"

I nodded again.

Still holding my chin, she leaned forward and kissed me passionately on the lips. I closed my eyes and allowed her tongue to flow into mine, enjoying its exploration of my mouth. My arms soon fall limply at my sides, again exposing my still pained tits.

After about twenty seconds she pulled her face back and again looked into my eyes.

"Has the stupid racist cunt learned her lesson yet?"

I shook my head....no.

Another cruel smile came over her face.

CHAPTER IV

"Over my knees!"

Slowly I rose from the floor and made to crawl onto her lap, but she quickly stopped me. When she pointed to my skirt, I knew what she first wanted. With only a moment of hesitation, I began sliding my dress down to my shoes, allowing my panties to quickly follow. My shoes and socks came off as well, so that only my wedding ring remained on my body. I left it on as I carefully laid myself over her gorgeous black legs. I delighted in the feel of my belly sliding over them until my ass was right below her. My breasts pressed uncomfortably against the bed covers as I awaited her next punishing desire.

But I would have to wait. While bracing for her swatting hand, it instead came to rest softly upon my cheeks. With delicateness only a woman can know, she began caressing my fleshing backside. I closed my eyes and enjoyed the gentle needing and gliding of her fingers, occasionally feeling her tickling nails on them.

"Tell me baby girl, when white lady was being mean to that poor black girl from school, was she secretly getting turned on?"

I didn't answer, not knowing exactly where this was coming from.

"Answer me baby girl. Were you getting off every time you and your snobby white bitches made fun of her?"

"Ye....yes...."

(SLAP) I gasped from the surprise of it all. Her hand had swiftly and quietly rose from my ass and came crashing back down hard. I had no idea how she knew. How could she tell I got turned on making fun of that bitch back then?

"I knew you did slut. I knew that white cunny of yours couldn't help but cream with power after humiliating a black girl. All you white women are the same, getting all hot thinking your better than us!" (SLAP!)

"OWWW....Mistress I'm sorry..."

(SLAP) "Shut up you pig! It's not your fault, it's in your blood. You can't help but be racist bitches. But that's the same reason why you got even hornier when she fought back wasn't it?" (SLAP)

I moaned painfully into the bed. My lack of an answer was evidence enough to her question. It was all true. I was a pretty white girl and she had been a low class black girl. I was supposed to be better than she was. I was raised TO be better. Yet with my neck helplessly trapped in her hand, my clothes powerless on the floor, I was at her mercy. This black girl could have had her way with me and that power washed me into submission.

(SLAP)

"It turned you on to have the tables turned. It got those tiny nubs all hard didn't it? It got that pink pussy all moist and wet being showed up by a black girl? Right Bitch?"

"YEESSSS MISTRESS!!!!"

(SLAP)(SLAP)(SLAP)

"But poor pathetic white lady wanted more didn't she? (SLAP) She wanted to be humiliated (SLAP) and abused (SLAP) and turned into a black girl's bitch (SLAP) Didn't she?"

"Yes Mistress PLEASE! Please make me your bitch! Abuse me, humiliate me. I deserve it so much. Please!!!!!!"

(SLAP)(SLAP)(SLAP)(SLAP).....

I lost count of the number of swats on my once white ass. All I knew was that I was fully reliving the experience of my mind. I was totally back in time, back in high school, behind in the fields. I was being completely stripped in front of my friends, imagining my ass getting swatted over and over by the black girl the way I've dreamt about for years since. I didn't care that my ass was on fire, or that I'd probably regret what I was allowing. I didn't care that it was a barely legal black prostitute giving me my pain or my punishment. I DIDNT CARE!

I had no idea when she actually stopped spanking my ass. I must have been kicking and crying on her lap for some time before I came to my senses. She had gone back to caressing my checks again. Despite being as soft and gentle as she had been earlier, my soar skin tingled in pain at every movement of her fingers, and I winced constantly.

Then my eyes went wide as her fingers slide off my cheeks to between my thighs. Encouraging me to widen my knees she was soon pressing against my cunt lips and, for the first time, I could feel the cool air over its wetness.

"This abuse really does turn you on doesn't it slut?"

I hid my face in the sheets in shame.

"Stand!"

CHAPTER V

I quickly scurried off her knees, intoxicated by the powerful command in her voice. In a second I was standing before her, tits red and ass sore.

"Spread your legs!"

I did as I was told. She paused for a moment, waiting for me to do so.

"Open your lips for me!"

My fingers trembled as I reached down and spread my oily sex for my black Mistress.

She leaned forward and examined me for a moment, staring into the pink displayed for her. Her eyes fixed upon my clit, proudly out for her to see as she lifted her right hand to it.

I quivered as two fingers slid up along my wet lips before resting on my hot bud. As she began rubbing my sensitive sex organ, I closed my eyes and allowed myself to enjoy the new wonderful sensations she was giving me. After a moment, her fingers were replaced by a thumb, the two fingers now entering into my very warm vagina. Before I knew it I was being fucked by her fingers right there in the middle of the room. I reopened my eyes and watched in awe as her fingers moved in and out of my cunny while her thumb teased my clit wild.

I struggle to remain standing as she moved faster and faster, my knees growing weak while sweat collected on my forehead. My fingers desperately trying to hold my lips apart as hers jam faster and faster into me. Then at the worst possible moment, they suddenly stopped. A wave of frustration came over me as my eyes flew to hers for an explanation as to why my Mistress had stopped my pleasure. Her fingers were still inside me, but were no longer moving.

"Fuck them Princess!"

For a moment I didn't move, not realizing what she was trying to tell me to do.

"Get that white ass moving! Fuck my fingers like the dumb bitch that you are!"

I bent my knees and pushed her fingers deeper into me, then quickly straightened back out. In a few more seconds I was fucking my puss on her fingers for all I was worth, crying with renewed pleasure.

Again I close my eyes and allow myself to imagine being in the back of the school. Both my friends now staring at me in shock and disgust as I passively lean against the wall while a black hand slips into the top of my skirt. The look of pleasure washing over my face as she dares to find my wet, submissive sex tucked safely away inside my panties. The look of absolute revolution on my friend's faces as I began to desperately fuck back.

"Lady, you truly are pathetic you know that?"

My eyes open again at her words, the illusion in my mind vanishing as I stare hungrily into her eyes. Gone were the images of school and friends. I was back to being a middle aged wife, fucking a black prostitute's slick fingers for four hundred dollars!

I moaned as I fucked even faster, rapidly thrusting my hips along her dark fingers like the absolute fool that I was. Even when her thumbnail began to scratch tormentingly against my clitty I didn't dare stop. All I could do was moan and buck my way closer and closer to desperate release.

Within another moment I had completely abandoned my attempts to hold my oily lips apart. Constantly they were slipping out of my grasp. Instead I shamefully brought one wet hand to my mouth and sucked my fingers while the other played with my still reddened tits. My legs felt as if they were on fire as the muscles in them worked to the point of collapse, thrusting my hips into her fingers.

"Is this what white sluts do when they let loose? Do they get off fucking their dirty cunts against black women's fingers? Is this how you demonstrate your superiority to a black woman, by fucking their fingers and paying for it?"

"YES MISTRESS!"

"What are you?"

This time there was no hesitation as I freely professed my degrading title: "I'm a Dirty Stupid White Racist Cunt!"

Suddenly her fingers pulled out of my juiced cunt to allow for the flurry of pussy slappings that immediately followed. I let out a cry of inhuman pain as I desperately thrusted out my pelvis to meet her swatting hand. In seconds pain and pleasure completely washed over me as I collapsed to the floor squealing like a pig, my body shaking and convulsing like a mad woman.

My Mistress just watched from the bed at the havoc she had caused my mind and body. The whole time it was with the widest grin. Don't even think of asking me how long I was cumming at her feet, only that it felt like the longest moments of my life.

At some point I managed to regain my senses and got back to my knees before her. Despite the stinging pain in my tits, ass, and pussy, my entire face had a glow to it. Never had I orgasmed like that before, and I had never ever gotten this close to living out my deepest fantasy. At times I really felt as if I were back at school, being dominated the way I ever so wished I could have been. I beamed up at my Mistress for giving this to me and she smiled warmly back, acknowledging me.

Yet her smile faded when she started to reach her arms forward to me. As she gently pressed her hands against my shoulders, I allowed her to be push me backwards until I was lying on my back. I passively laid there, watching as she stood and walked along to my side, until she was standing next to my resting head. Lifting one leg, she placed it over me and onto the other side of my face.

Now I had no choice but to look up, past her pretty calves, past her cute knees, past her firm thighs, up her micro skirt where her dark hairless lips lay. I could just barely make out its outline and I realized it had never even occurred to me that she wouldn't have any panties on.

She looked down at me for a brief moment, seemingly enjoying the stance she now had over me. Then unceremoniously she lifted her skirt up to her waist. For the first time in my life, I was looking at another woman's very wet sex. I could see it glistening above me as I looked at it as if I were in a trance. It took me a moment before I realized that she was lowering her hips to my face.

I barely had time to think as my head was soon encased between her two strong black thighs. My eyes went wide when my lips pressed right against her sex lips. Instantly the smell of sex filled my nostrils. The smell of countless past customers filling my lungs. Her juices, which still managed to force their way past my closed lips, carried the faint taste of male seed.

I moaned into her pussy for her to get off, fully realizing the depravity of my new position.

"Open those prissy lips bitch. Stick that tongue up inside me." She ordered, yet my lips and tongue still didn't move. This wasn't what I had wanted. I didn't want to taste the filth that lay inside her. I was no longer thinking about my high school days as a snobbish white girl. I was totally focused on the fact that I was being asked to clean out a whore's used pussy! This isn't what I had paid her for.

Reaching back, she took hold of my soar right breast and cruelly squeezed. "I said eat me you fucking dyke! Suck my pussy like the fucking white lesb slut that you are!"

I opened my mouth to scream from the pain surging from my tit and unknowingly allowed more of her tainted juices to flow into my mouth, coating my tongue and teeth. Yet I still didn't eat her, causing her to reach back her other hand to squeeze both my poor breasts even harder.

With a muffled scream I darted my tongue out into her warm, moist hole desperate to stop the pain. Instantly she clenched her thighs hard around my head and encouraged my tongue.

"Goooood girl. Good white girl. Clean that black pussy you love so much. Suck out all the nasties inside. Be a good little maid to my little pussy."

Having little choice in the matter I began to clean her used cunt. Despite my initial revulsion, I resolved myself to sucking the remnants of her former paying customers into my mouth. I could tell she was relishing every moment of this. Not every day does she have a white woman between her well fucked thighs, and tonight she was most likely living out her own dark fantasies at my expense, literally.

All my attention was now centered on her cunt. I kind of lost myself as I did my best to satisfy her. Forgetting eventually how filthy the liquids pouring into my mouth were. Instead I tongued her folds and walls as she demanded. Every once in awhile she would reach back and slap my breasts to make me pay more attention.

By the time she finally fell off my numb face, she had orgasmed three times, and my throat and belly were coated with stuff I really DONT want to think about.

We both laid on the hotel room floor for some time, not moving a single muscle as we tried to regain our energy. I honestly don't think I could have talked if I wanted to, as my tongue lay slack in my mouth. The whole time her fingers lightly played with my still erect nipples as we panted next to each other.

I'm guessing that due to her youth, she was able to regain her energy faster than I. I watched from the floor as she eventually stood, composing herself in only the way a prostitute could.

Disappearing into the bathroom, supposedly to check her hair and make up, she soon came back out and looked at me for a moment, still lying on the cheap carpet floor. My face covered in her mixed juices, my soar pinkish breasts throbbing on my heaving chest.

Turning towards the sofa, she caught sight of my purse resting on it and made her way to it. Opening it up, she ruffled inside for a moment. I wanted to say something to her, but couldn't. Finally she pulled her hand back out, clutching another two hundred dollars.

"I think a tip is in order don't you Miss?"

I said nothing, just watched as she stuffed the bills into her cleavage like before.

We spent a few more hours together that night. Some of it was spent licking and sucking her toes as she rested on the bed, regaining her strength. She also enjoyed giving my butt yet another spanking before ordering me to fuck my clitty against her toes to orgasm. At first I felt like a complete idiot for doing it, but after a little bit I was fucking them like a complete slut. Of course I had to lick each toe clean again after I did.

Despite being totally degraded and used by a prostitute, I have never felt so content and so alive as I did that night. Its not every day one gets to live out a childhood fantasy in such a fashion and this girl knew exactly what I wanted, some how.

Eventually I made my way into the shower to wash up. When I came back out, she patiently waited for me to get dressed, enjoying the wincing of my face each time cloths touched a sore part of my body. Twenty minutes later we were back outside and in my SUV, heading towards her familiar street corner. The whole drive we didn't say a word to each other.

When we finally arrived, she casually got out and closed the door behind her. Turning she look at me with that same evil smile, sending chills down my spine and centering in my pussy. I lowered the window.

"I must admit you've been the easiest, and most enjoyable trick I've ever had."

I didn't know whether to say thank you or not.

"Waking up this morning, I never expected to get paid to abuse a white chicks body. But kudos to you babe. If you've got any fellow horny racist bitches you know of, by all means send them my way!"

"Um....ok...." I seriously doubted any of my friends harbored my same degrading fantasies. Then again...."

"What are you?" She commanded, still with the evil, seductive grin. I blushed as several other prostitutes took notice.

"I'm...."

"WHAT ARE YOU?"

I look down at the passenger seat: "I'm a stupid racist white cunt!"

Several of the other girls paused in mid-step as they no doubt heard my humiliating admission. But I didn't dare look at any of them, even after I heard a few giggles.

"That you are baby girl, that you are. See you around lady."

And like that she turned and strode off down the street looking for the next roaming car. That's all I really was to her, another trick. A second later my car turned the corner and she was out of sight. Less than an hour later I was back home. Back where no one would ever want to hurt me. Back in the place where love was free and unconditional. Back where black girls never dared enter to punish me. I was Home!

Removing my cloths I carefully slipped beside my husband into bed, wrapping my arms around his sleeping body. My breasts ached as they pressed against his bare back, reminding me of how they got that way. A smile crept across my face and a tingling formed between my thighs before I fell into a blissful, content sleep. A sleep filled with new dreams of stupid racist white bitches getting exactly what they deserve by sexy black vixens.

END